Earl of Sandwich

My name is Seymour Sleuth. I am the world's greatest detective. With my assistant and photographer, Abbott Muggs, I travel around the world solving mysteries. This is the casebook of one of my most puzzling mysteries. I call it <u>The Mystery of the Monkey's Maze.</u>

The Mystery of the Monkey's Maze

story and pictures by
Doug Cushman

Edible plant
from Borneo—
YUM!

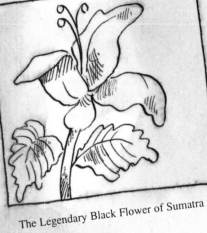

The Legendary Black Flower of Sumatra

BLACK FLOWER— FACT OR FICTION?

by Maggie Snoop

Most people think that the Black Flower of Sumatra is only a legend. One person, however, believes that it really exists. That person is the great explorer Dr. Irene A. Tann. Along with this reporter, she and a team of dedicated experts will travel to Borneo to discover if the legend is true. I will (see page 3)

■ HarperCollinsPublishers

February 23, 2:26 P.M.; Singapore— Muggs and I are here in Singapore to enter the Great Curry Cooking Contest. As we practice my famous Mystery Rice Curry with Peanut Butter and Pickles, a messenger delivers a note to our hotel room.

PONGO PH🌴 HOTEL

SINGAPORE • TOKYO • HACKENSACK

Dear Detective Sleuth,
My mother, the great explorer
Dr. Irene A. Tann, is in danger.
You are the only one who can
help! Please meet me in the
hotel lobby in one hour. I have
no one else to turn to!
                    Maurice Tann

Same day, 3:35 P.M.— Muggs and I meet with Maurice Tann. I order a light snack and ask him why he needs my help.

"I have just returned from the rain forest in Borneo," he says. "I am helping my mother look for the legendary Black Flower of Sumatra. We believe it can cure hiccups forever! Most people do not think it really exists. If we find it, it would be a great discovery.

"But someone is causing us trouble. Much of our food has disappeared. Someone put sand in the sugar bowl and tied knots in our underwear. And two days ago, my mother received a scary note. Someone is trying to scare us away. Please, you must help us!"

GoaWay!

Note to myself: Smudges on note look familiar. Chocolate perhaps?

February 23, 4:45 P.M. — I agree to take the case. Muggs will join us to photograph every step of this mystery. Maurice books us on a flight to Borneo. I suggest we take a comfortable and safe boat, but Maurice insists a plane will be faster.

February 24, 6:16 A.M.; Borneo—After a long flight, we arrive on the island of Borneo. Elephants take us into the jungle to Dr. Tann's camp.

Same day, 7:23 A.M.—Our journey through the jungle is long and bumpy. I'm beginning to get hungry. Maybe we can find a snack?

My elephant helps me look for something to eat.

Same day, 12:15 P.M.; Dr. Tann's camp — We arrive at the camp and meet Dr. Tann. She looks scared.

"I just got another note!" she cries.

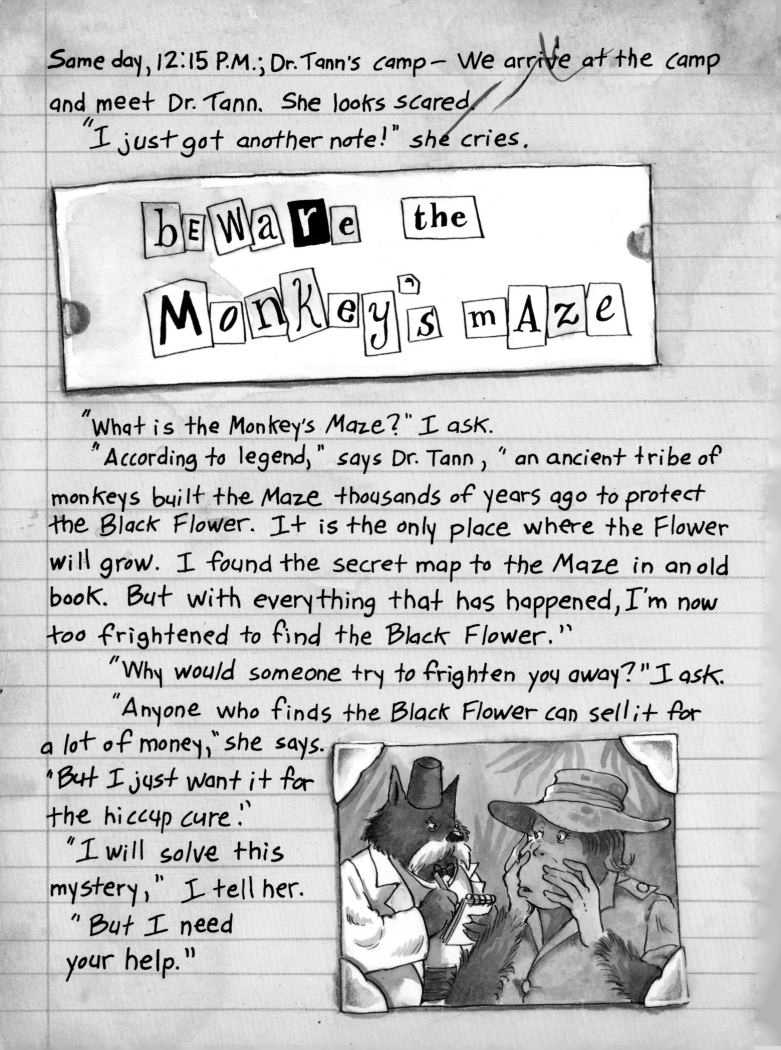

beWare the MonKey's mAze

"What is the Monkey's Maze?" I ask.

"According to legend," says Dr. Tann, "an ancient tribe of monkeys built the Maze thousands of years ago to protect the Black Flower. It is the only place where the Flower will grow. I found the secret map to the Maze in an old book. But with everything that has happened, I'm now too frightened to find the Black Flower."

"Why would someone try to frighten you away?" I ask.

"Anyone who finds the Black Flower can sell it for a lot of money," she says. "But I just want it for the hiccup cure."

"I will solve this mystery," I tell her. "But I need your help."

Muggs and I search Dr. Tann's hut for clues. Muggs takes pictures of what we find.

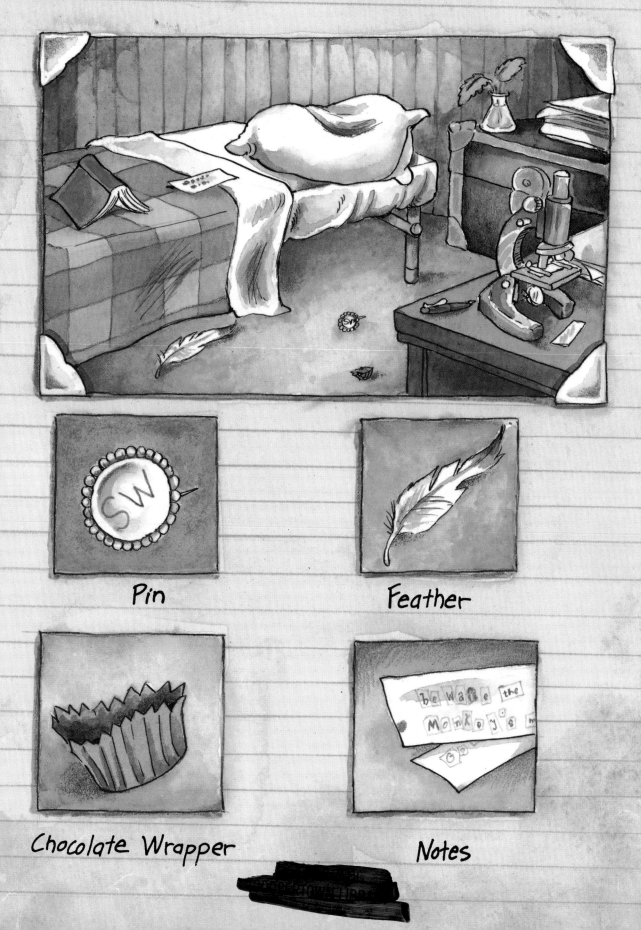

Pin

Feather

Chocolate Wrapper

Notes

February 24, 1:27 P.M.—Only three people live here in camp with Dr. Tann. Is one of them trying to scare her away?

Timbol

A jungle guide.
He lives in Borneo.
He knows the rain forest
very well.

Maggie Snoop

A reporter. She is writing
an article about the Black
Flower for her newspaper,
The London Tattletale.

Silo Wiggit

Dr. Tann's assistant.
He has been with
Dr. Tann for one week.

February 24, 2:17 P.M. — Muggs and I meet Timbol outside his hut.
He is feeding his parrot. (He does not offer to feed me!)
"I don't think the Flower exists," he tells me. "Dr. Tann
is wasting her time. These people don't belong here in the
jungle. I'm glad someone is trying to scare them away."
"Then why are you trying to help her find the
Flower?" I ask.
"I need the money", he says. "I have to feed my
elephants and parrot. They eat lots of fruit, just like
me. Now go away and leave me alone!"

A feather
from Timbol's
parrot

Could he be the one
writing the notes?

February 24, 3:06 P.M.—I interview Maggie Snoop in her hut. She is eating chocolates. (She doesn't offer me any!)

"Of course I think the Flower is real," she says. "I am writing a <u>wonderful</u> article about Dr. Tann and the Flower. You see, I am a <u>wonderful</u> writer. I have written all these <u>wonderful</u> stories." She points to a stack of newspapers. "But writing does not make me rich. I need lots of money to buy all the <u>wonderful</u> fancy things I want."

"If you found the Flower first, you would be rich," I say.

"Yes," says Maggie. "That would be <u>wonderful</u>, wouldn't it?"

Since 1846 · FINE CHOCOLATE · FANCY · Since 1846

Label from box of Chocolates

Feather from Maggie's hat

Could the chocolate smudges on the notes have come from Maggie?

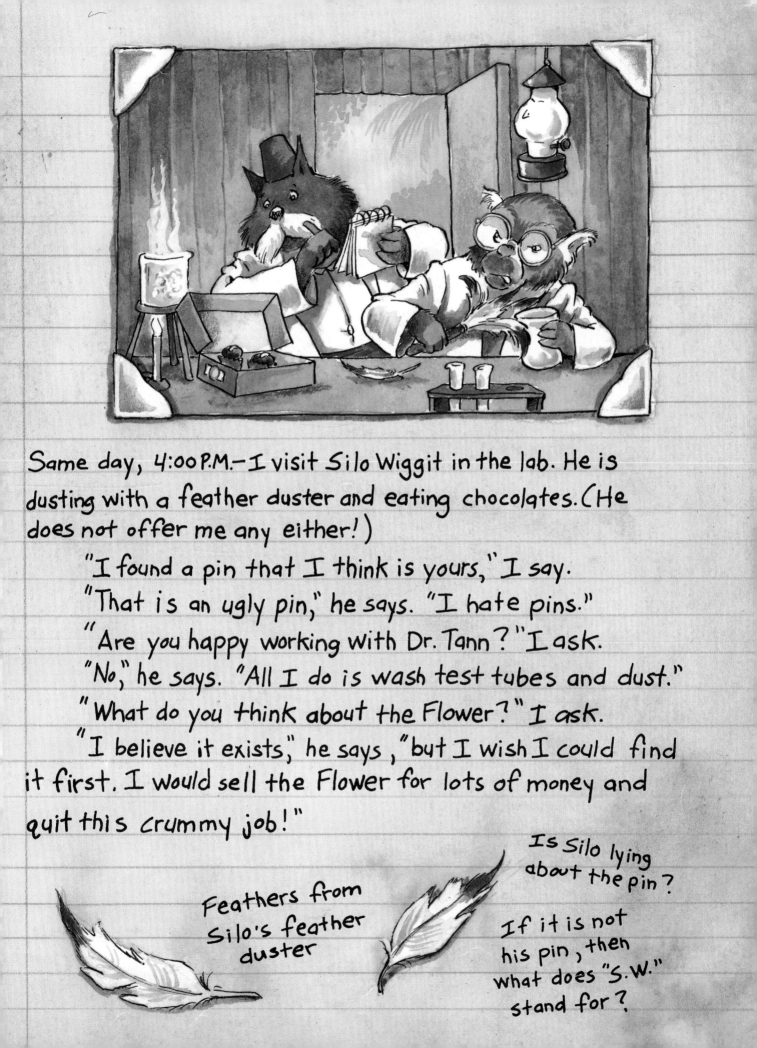

Same day, 4:00 P.M.— I visit Silo Wiggit in the lab. He is dusting with a feather duster and eating chocolates. (He does not offer me any either!)

"I found a pin that I think is yours," I say.

"That is an ugly pin," he says. "I hate pins."

"Are you happy working with Dr. Tann?" I ask.

"No," he says. "All I do is wash test tubes and dust."

"What do you think about the Flower?" I ask.

"I believe it exists," he says, "but I wish I could find it first. I would sell the Flower for lots of money and quit this crummy job!"

Feathers from Silo's feather duster

Is Silo lying about the pin?

If it is not his pin, then what does "S.W." stand for?

February 24, 6:18 P.M.— I return to my hut. Dr. Tann rushes in.

"Another note just arrived!" she cries. "And the map to the Maze has been stolen! Now anyone can find the Flower! I give up!"

"Don't give up yet," I tell her. "It's too dark now for <u>anyone</u> to go out into the jungle and look for the Flower. We have time until it's morning. I think we can solve this mystery by then."

STAY AWAY FROM THE MONKEY'S MAZE or ELSE!

Same day, 7:47 P.M. — Muggs and I study my notes over a light dinner. Something is not right, but I don't know what. Is someone lying? Perhaps I should look at the clues from another angle.

Notes on the Clues

FEATHER
- does not match feather from Timbol's parrot
- matches feather from Maggie's hat
- matches feather from Silo's feather duster

PIN
- matches letters in Silo Wiggit's name
- looks very fancy

CHOCOLATE WRAPPER
- Timbol eats only fruit
- Maggie Snoop likes chocolate
- Silo Wiggit likes chocolate

THE NOTES
- made from letters cut from newspapers
- smudges on them look like chocolate

Notes on the Suspects

TIMBOL
- eats only fruit
- wants money for fruit for parrot and elephants
- does not think Flower exists

MAGGIE SNOOP
- eats chocolate
- wants money to buy fancy things
- believes Flower is real
- has newspapers in her hut

SILO WIGGIT
- eats chocolate
- wants money to quit his crummy job
- believes Flower is real
- letters on pin match his name

February 25, midnight — I cannot sleep. This case is difficult to solve. My stomach is making noises. I get up to look for a small midnight snack. I knock over a table and scatter the clues. Some fall upside down.

"Of course!" I cry out. "What a silly detective I am. I know who wrote the notes!"

I wake up Maurice and Dr. Tann. They agree to come with me and confront the note writer.

We hurry to the hut of...

Maggie Snoop! She is caught making another note
using her own newspapers!

Maggie tries to run away...

... but she is easily caught.

February 25, 1:30 A.M.— The jungle police take Maggie to jail. I make a statement to the police. Dr. Tann is no longer frightened. She can now find the Maze — and the Black Flower!

Confession Form

I, Maggie Snoop, wrote all the notes to scare Dr. Tann away from her camp. I stole some of the food, put sand in the sugar bowl, tied knots in the underwear, and stole the map to the Maze. I wanted to find the Black Flower myself so I could sell it for a lot of money and buy lots of fancy things.

Maggie Snoop

Statement Form 92-EZ

I, Detective Seymour Sleuth, used my highly intelligent brain to solve this mystery. When the pin fell upside down, I realized the letters "S W" could also read "M S," the same letters in Maggie Snoop's name. I knew Maggie liked fancy things. Silo would not wear such a fancy pin. The pin must belong to Maggie. The notes were made of letters cut from Maggie's newspapers and were smudged with chocolate, Maggie's favorite treat. Maggie must have dropped the pin and the feather from her hat when she delivered the first letter to Dr. Tann's hut. It is not surprising I solved this mystery so quickly. After all, I am the greatest detective in the world!

Fingerprint file for Maggie Snoop   no. 3726

right hoof   left hoof   nose

So far this was a strange case. But the strangest part was yet to come!

February 25, 6:30 A.M.— After a few hours' sleep, Dr. Tann, Maurice, Silo, and Timbol come to my hut. "We are finally going to use the map to find the Maze," says Dr. Tann. "Would you and Muggs like to come along?"

Muggs and I agree to join them, even though they won't wait to eat a hearty breakfast.

Map through the jungle to the Maze

Note to myself:
Remember to bring
food!

Same day, 9:24 A.M.; Somewhere in the jungle—After a long trip through the jungle, we find the entrance to the Monkey's Maze. Dr. Tann says that there should be a map of the Maze itself somewhere on one of the walls. They all hunt for the map. I hunt for something to eat.

February 25, 9:35 A.M. — The map of the Maze has been found! It is carved on a wall, hidden under some vines. It shows us how to get to the center of the Maze where the Black Flower grows. It also shows some of the dangers we may encounter along the way. The others want to go immediately. I think we should wait until after lunchtime.

Same day, 10:00 A.M. — I suggest that everyone follow me. My expert memory and sense of direction will get us through the Maze quickly.

Same day, 10:05 A.M. — We are hopelessly lost.

We meet with some of the dangers of the Maze.
My bravery keeps everyone calm.

February 25, 12:13 P.M.— Timbol finds the way to the center of the Maze. At last we find the Black Flower of Sumatra! Now we can prove it really exists. Dr. Tann is very happy. She begins to dig it up. Suddenly we hear a sound.

"Look!" she says. "Something lives under the Flower. It's an animal! I have never seen anything like it before. We cannot take away its home. Muggs can take lots of pictures for the museum, but the Flower should stay here in the jungle, where it belongs. We can take a few seeds to grow our own flower for the hiccup cure."

Dr. Tann and Maurice are happy. Silo has some seeds to grow a flower, so he is happy. Muggs has taken lots of pictures, so he is happy. We return to camp. I eat a big lunch. I am very happy.

March 1, 10:35 A.M. — We prepare to leave for home. As I finish packing, one of the elephants helps me with my trunk.

Note: I will never again trust an elephant with a trunk.

photo credit: Abbott Muggs

EXPLORER DISCOVERS NEW ANIMAL

Borneo—Famous explorer Dr. Irene A. Tann has discovered a new animal in the rain forest of Borneo.

"It was a complete surprise," said Dr. Tann. "I had just found the legendary Black Flower of Sumatra when I saw the animal. This is indeed an exciting discovery."

With her was the famous detective Seymour Sleuth. Detective Sleuth had just solved a difficult case. He was unable to comment, however, as he had just taken a big bite of (see page 3, col. 4)

The Mystery of the Monkey's Maze
Copyright © 1999 by Doug Cushman
Printed in the U.S.A. All rights reserved.
http://www.harperchildrens.com

Library of Congress Cataloging-in-Publication Data
Cushman, Doug.
    The mystery of the monkey's maze / story and pictures by Doug Cushman.
       p.   cm.
    Summary: The great detective Seymour Sleuth and his photographer Muggs travel to Borneo to help find the legendary Black Flower of Sumatra, a possible cure for the hiccups.
    ISBN 0-06-027719-X. — ISBN 0-06-027720-3 (lib. bdg.)
    [1. Mystery and detective stories. 2. Borneo—Fiction.] I. Title.
PZ7.C959Mye 1999   98-39424
[E]—dc21   CIP
                                                              AC

1 2 3 4 5 6 7 8 9 10
First Edition

AIR

FOR JACKIE
24
WITH LOVE

5¢